Last Voyage of the *S.S. Panglossian*

Matt Kambic and Matthew Kennedy

chalk hill publishing

prologue ~ **The Book of Unknown Hope**
A SMALL, FROG-LIKE SPACE VESSEL, *THE S.S. PANGLOSSIAN*, KICKS ITS WAY OUTWARD FROM THE MILKY WAY GALAXY. THOUGH IT APPEARS TO BE MOVING SLOWLY, IT IS TRAVELING AT NEAR LIGHT SPEED TOWARDS THE EDGE OF THE KNOWN UNIVERSE, A BARRIER CALCULATED WITH PRECISION IN **2250**. THIS BARRIER, NOW KNOWN AS THE **X-WALL**, PROVED TO BE MUCH CLOSER THAN PREVIOUSLY EXPECTED **AND**- OMINOUSLY- MIGHT BE COLLAPSING INWARD, TOWARDS EARTH. HAS THE **BIG BANG** FINALLY EXPENDED ITS ENERGIES AND BEGUN ITS THEORIZED REVERSAL? IS THIS AN INSTRUMENTATION ERROR, OR A PREFACE TO THE LAST, AND GREATEST, CALAMITY? THE PANGLOSSIAN IS ON ITS WAY TO GATHER DATA, SEEK ANSWERS, AND EXPLORE INTO THIS **GREATEST BEYOND**.

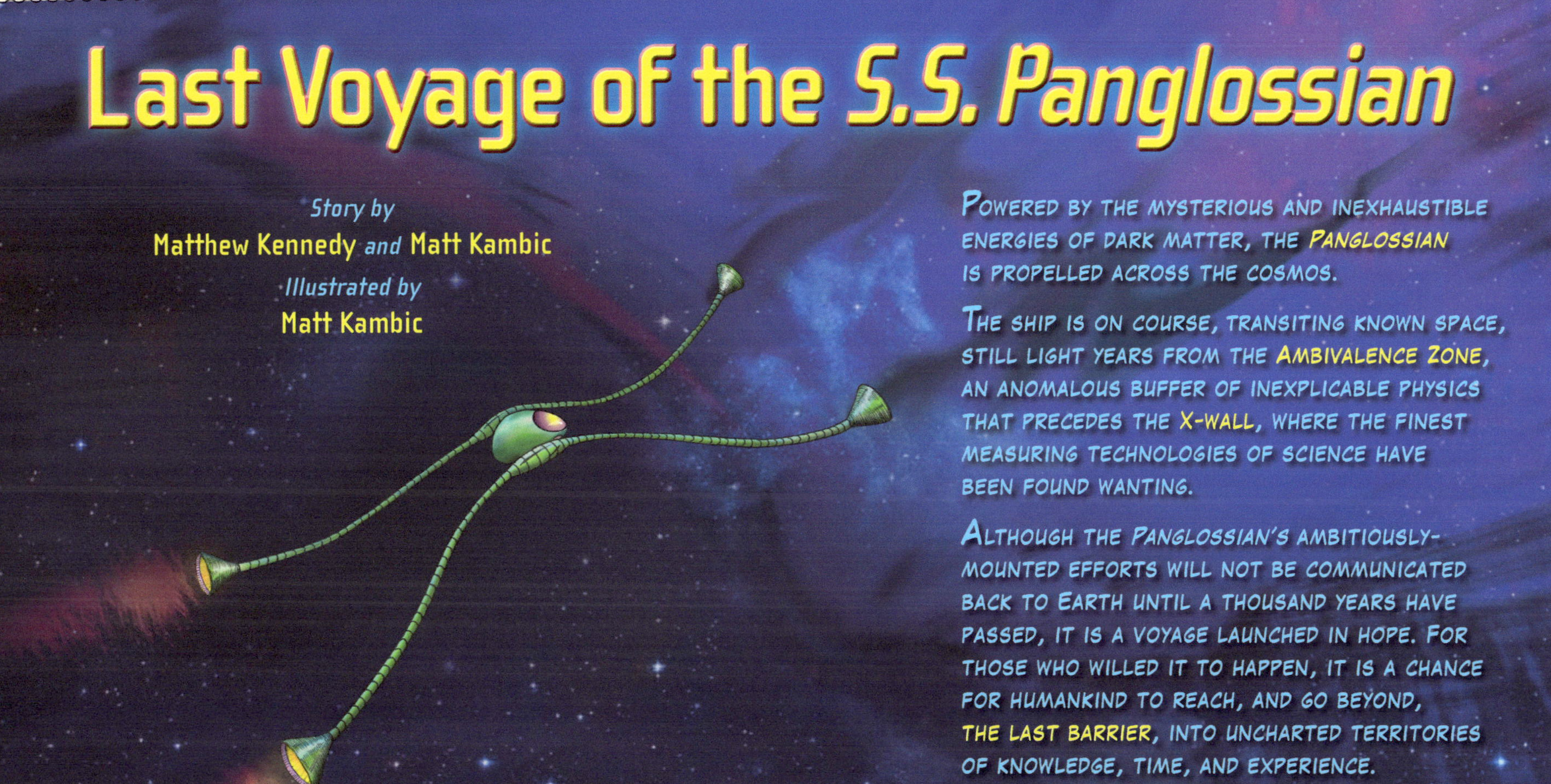

In the Optimists Society's Commons Room, the mood is upbeat. The Panglossian is on her way.
It's a marvelous feeling to share, Roaringman. We're the new Magellans. That said, it's better they don't know about the potential collapse. If they did, there'd be far fewer smiles around the table.
We haven't confirmed what you're suggesting, Dr. Onox. That the universe is collapsing. Folding in on itself. The Earth, all of us...
...we'd be like eggs in a crushing machine. Squeezed by gravity til all life is nothing but a memory.
Stay optimistic, Roaringman. The Panglossian's mission is fascinating. We're in the land of theory. And, personally, though we won't live to see its outcome, I'm a member of this Society for good reason. I simply can't believe the whole of existence is about to be concluded.
Though I admit, as Leonard Cohen once said, I could be wrong.

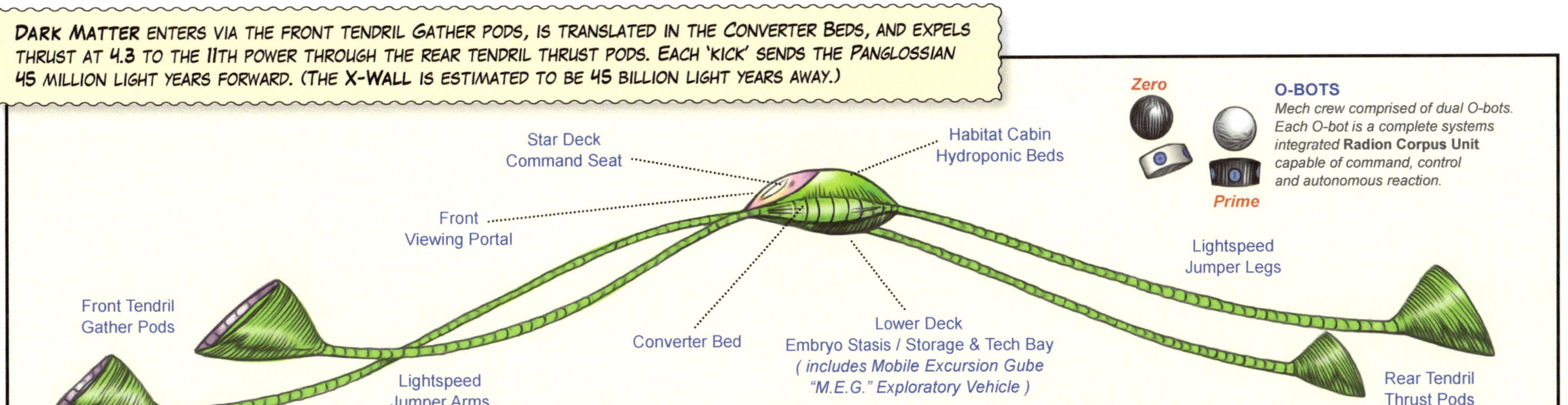

DARK MATTER ENTERS VIA THE FRONT TENDRIL GATHER PODS, IS TRANSLATED IN THE CONVERTER BEDS, AND EXPELS THRUST AT 4.3 TO THE 11TH POWER THROUGH THE REAR TENDRIL THRUST PODS. EACH 'KICK' SENDS THE PANGLOSSIAN 45 MILLION LIGHT YEARS FORWARD. (THE X-WALL IS ESTIMATED TO BE 45 BILLION LIGHT YEARS AWAY.)
Star Deck
Command Seat
Habitat Cabin
Hydroponic Beds
Front
Viewing Portal
Front Tendril
Gather Pods
Lightspeed
Jumper Arms
Converter Bed
Lower Deck
Embryo Stasis / Storage & Tech Bay
(includes Mobile Excursion Gube
"M.E.G." Exploratory Vehicle)
Lightspeed
Jumper Legs
Rear Tendril
Thrust Pods
Zero
Prime
O-BOTS
Mech crew comprised of dual O-bots. Each O-bot is a complete systems integrated Radion Corpus Unit capable of command, control and autonomous reaction.

A SINGLE HUMAN EMBRYO LIES IN STASIS WITHIN THE SHIP'S CARBON-FACILE IMPLEMENTOR. BECAUSE THE JOURNEY WILL TAKE 1000 YEARS, THE EMBRYO WILL BE BIRTHED 30 YEARS PRIOR TO JOURNEY'S END. THIS SOLE HUMAN, TRAINED FOR 3 DECADES, WILL ULTIMATELY WITNESS AND REPORT ON CONDITIONS AT THE X-WALL, AND REPERCUSSIONS THAT MAY DICTATE THE FATE OF THE UNIVERSE.

THE SHIP CARRIES TWO SETS OF ENTANGLED PARTICLES. ONE SERVES AS AN ATOMIC BANDWIDTH OF INSTANTANEOUS COMMUNICATION WITH EARTH.
THE SECOND WILL FACILITATE COMMUNICATIONS BETWEEN THE PANGLOSSIAN AND THE HUMAN AS THE HUMAN NEGOTIATES THE FINAL SPACES BETWEEN THE SHIP, THE UNIVERSE, AND BEYOND.

THE S.S. ASTONISHED MOTHERSHIP CARRIED THE PANGLOSSIAN INTO THE GALAXY'S OUTER BELT. FROM THERE, IT WAS CATAPULTED FORTH~ WITH MUCH FANFARE AND OPTIMISM~ BEGINNING ITS 365,000 DAY JOURNEY INTO THE UNKNOWN, HUMANKIND'S KEEN AUDACITY AND DEEP APPREHENSIONS COMBINED INTO A GLORIOUS FORCE OF ENERGIES.
KICK BY KICK THE STARSHIP ADVANCED, CONSUMING LIGHT YEARS IN MASSIVE GULPS. ONBOARD SYSTEMS, ENGINEERED WITH GREAT CARE, PERFORMED UNFAILINGLY; LIFE SUSTENANCE, NAVIGATION, HYDROPONICS, DARK PROPELLANT EQUILIBRIUM, COLLISION THREAT WARNING TELEMETRY, AND HULL INTEGRITY MONITORING. THE TWIN O-BOTS, ZERO AND PRIME, RESTED SECURELY IN THEIR ANCHORING HARNESSES, BOTH POWERED DOWN AND OFFLINE.
THE EMBRYO SECURED IN STASIS, THE SHIP MOVED EVER OUTWARD, AS THE HUMANS WHO HAD SENT IT BY DEGREES PASSED AWAY, THEIR DESCENDANTS NOW THE EARTHBOUND PURVEYORS OF WHATEVER INFORMATION IT WOULD REPORT.

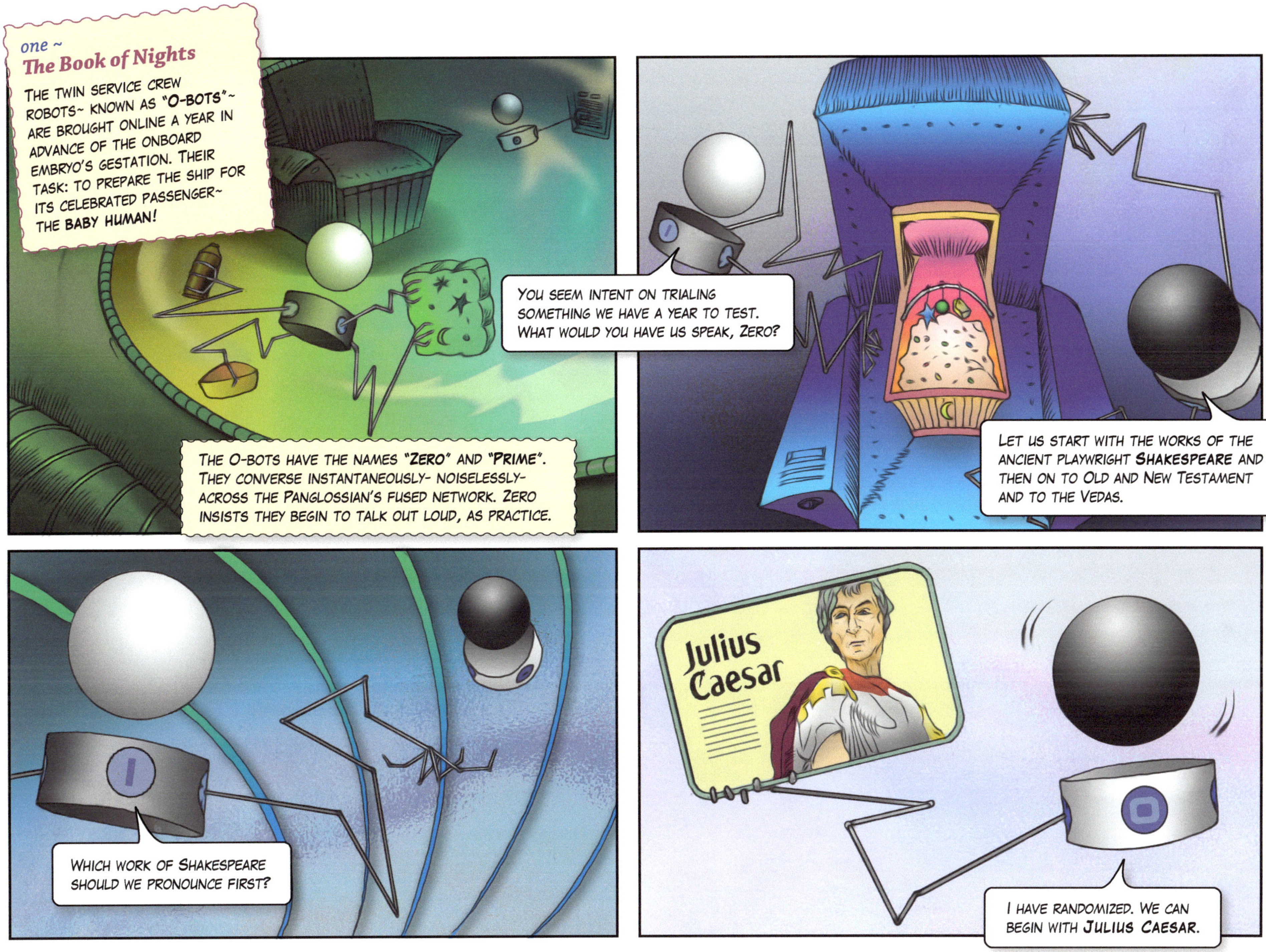

one ~
The Book of Nights
THE TWIN SERVICE CREW ROBOTS~ KNOWN AS "O-BOTS"~ ARE BROUGHT ONLINE A YEAR IN ADVANCE OF THE ONBOARD EMBRYO'S GESTATION. THEIR TASK: TO PREPARE THE SHIP FOR ITS CELEBRATED PASSENGER~ THE BABY HUMAN!
THE O-BOTS HAVE THE NAMES "ZERO" AND "PRIME". THEY CONVERSE INSTANTANEOUSLY~ NOISELESSLY~ ACROSS THE PANGLOSSIAN'S FUSED NETWORK. ZERO INSISTS THEY BEGIN TO TALK OUT LOUD, AS PRACTICE.
YOU SEEM INTENT ON TRIALING SOMETHING WE HAVE A YEAR TO TEST. WHAT WOULD YOU HAVE US SPEAK, ZERO?
LET US START WITH THE WORKS OF THE ANCIENT PLAYWRIGHT SHAKESPEARE AND THEN ON TO OLD AND NEW TESTAMENT AND TO THE VEDAS.

WHICH WORK OF SHAKESPEARE SHOULD WE PRONOUNCE FIRST?

Julius Caesar
I HAVE RANDOMIZED. WE CAN BEGIN WITH JULIUS CAESAR.

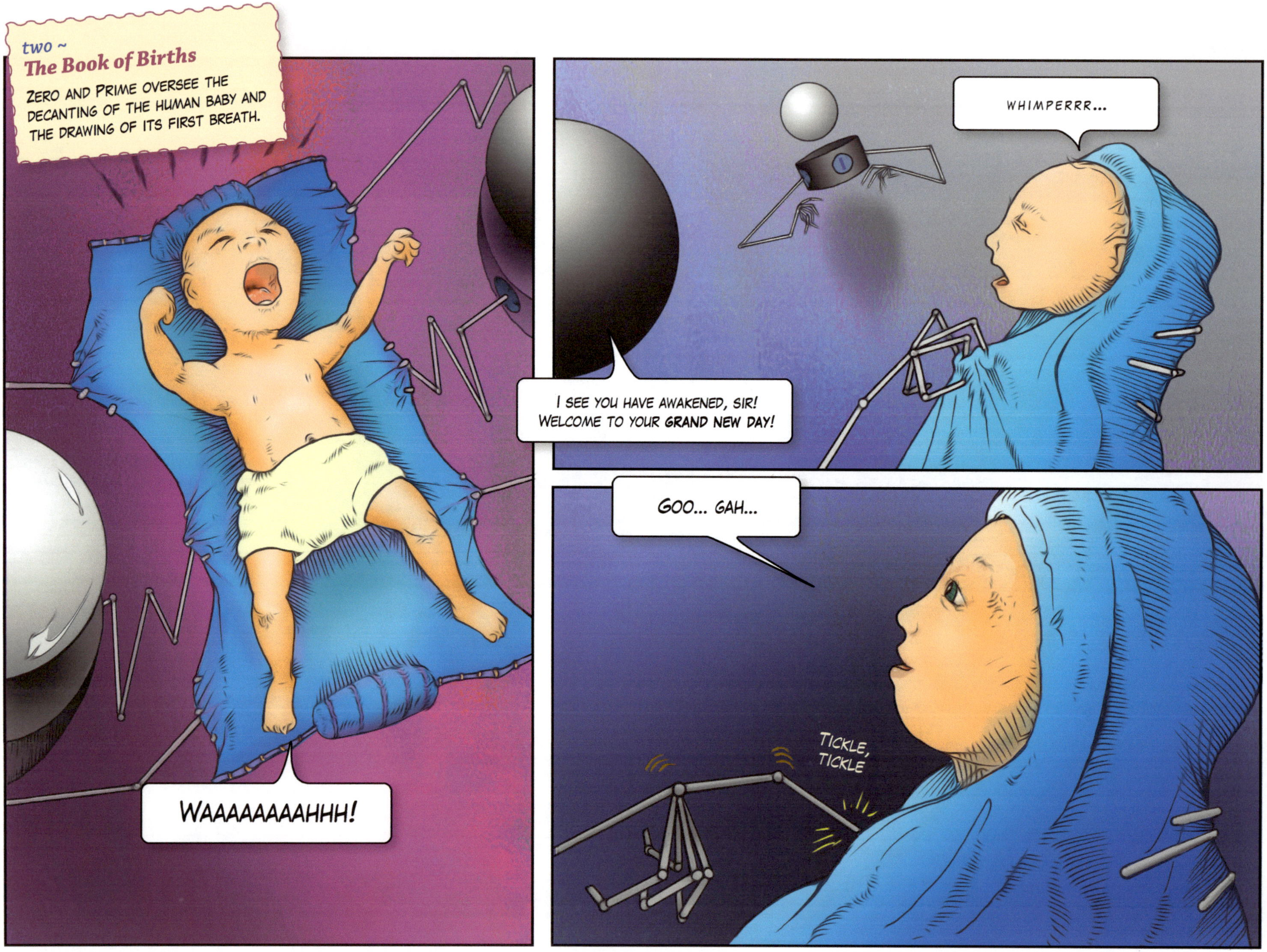

two

The Book of Births

ZERO AND PRIME OVERSEE THE DECANTING OF THE HUMAN BABY AND THE DRAWING OF ITS FIRST BREATH.

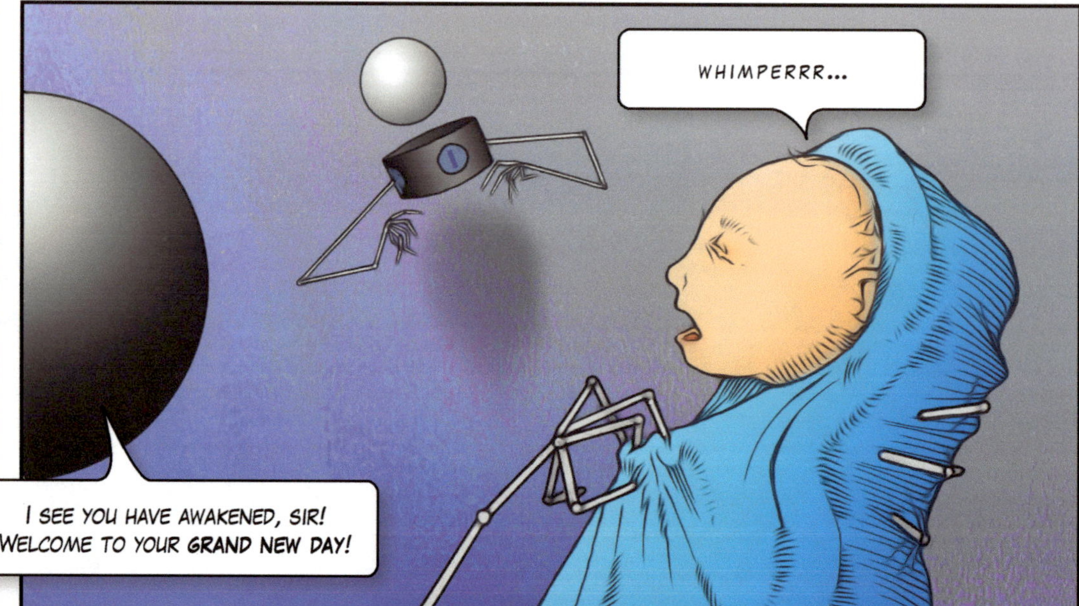

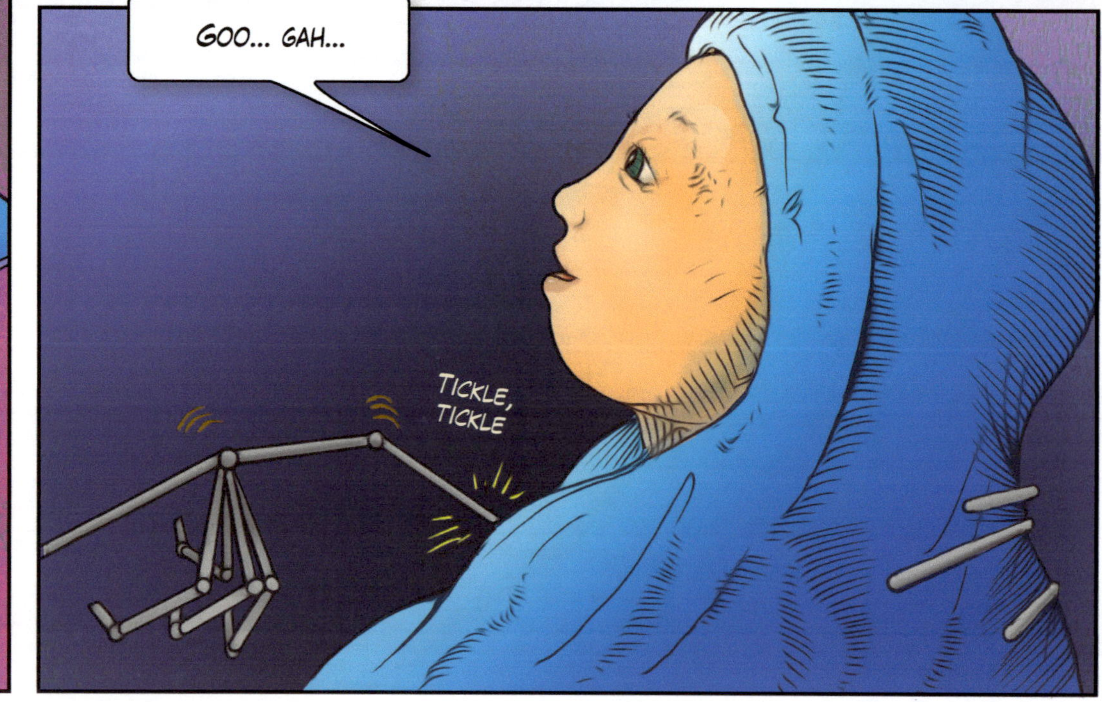

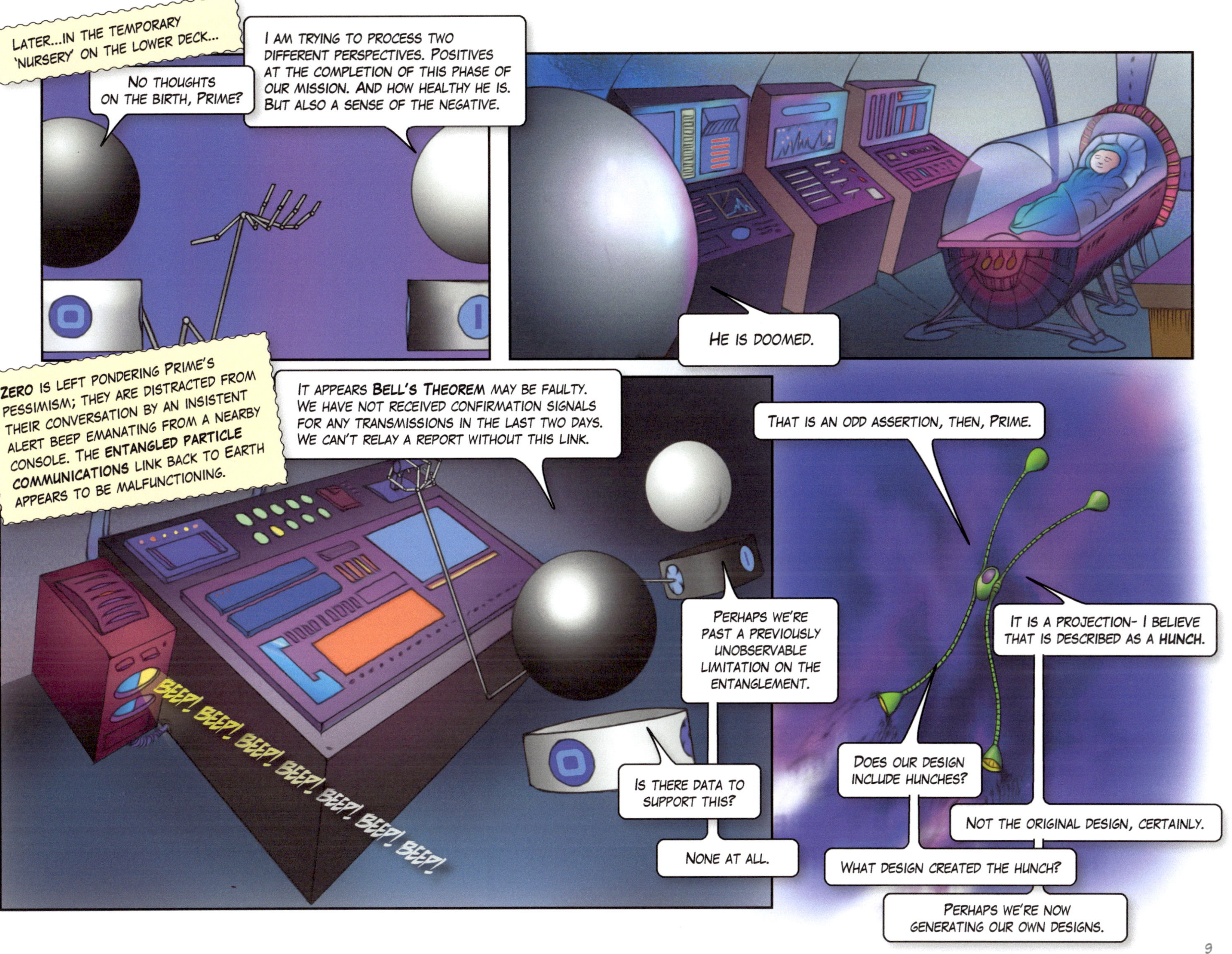

LATER...IN THE TEMPORARY 'NURSERY' ON THE LOWER DECK...
NO THOUGHTS ON THE BIRTH, PRIME?
I AM TRYING TO PROCESS TWO DIFFERENT PERSPECTIVES. POSITIVES AT THE COMPLETION OF THIS PHASE OF OUR MISSION. AND HOW HEALTHY HE IS. BUT ALSO A SENSE OF THE NEGATIVE.
HE IS DOOMED.
ZERO IS LEFT PONDERING PRIME'S PESSIMISM; THEY ARE DISTRACTED FROM THEIR CONVERSATION BY AN INSISTENT ALERT BEEP EMANATING FROM A NEARBY CONSOLE. THE ENTANGLED PARTICLE COMMUNICATIONS LINK BACK TO EARTH APPEARS TO BE MALFUNCTIONING.
IT APPEARS BELL'S THEOREM MAY BE FAULTY. WE HAVE NOT RECEIVED CONFIRMATION SIGNALS FOR ANY TRANSMISSIONS IN THE LAST TWO DAYS. WE CAN'T RELAY A REPORT WITHOUT THIS LINK.
THAT IS AN ODD ASSERTION, THEN, PRIME.
BEEP! BEEP! BEEP! BEEP! BEEP! BEEP!
PERHAPS WE'RE PAST A PREVIOUSLY UNOBSERVABLE LIMITATION ON THE ENTANGLEMENT.
IT IS A PROJECTION- I BELIEVE THAT IS DESCRIBED AS A HUNCH.
IS THERE DATA TO SUPPORT THIS?
DOES OUR DESIGN INCLUDE HUNCHES?
NOT THE ORIGINAL DESIGN, CERTAINLY.
NONE AT ALL.
WHAT DESIGN CREATED THE HUNCH?
PERHAPS WE'RE NOW GENERATING OUR OWN DESIGNS.

9

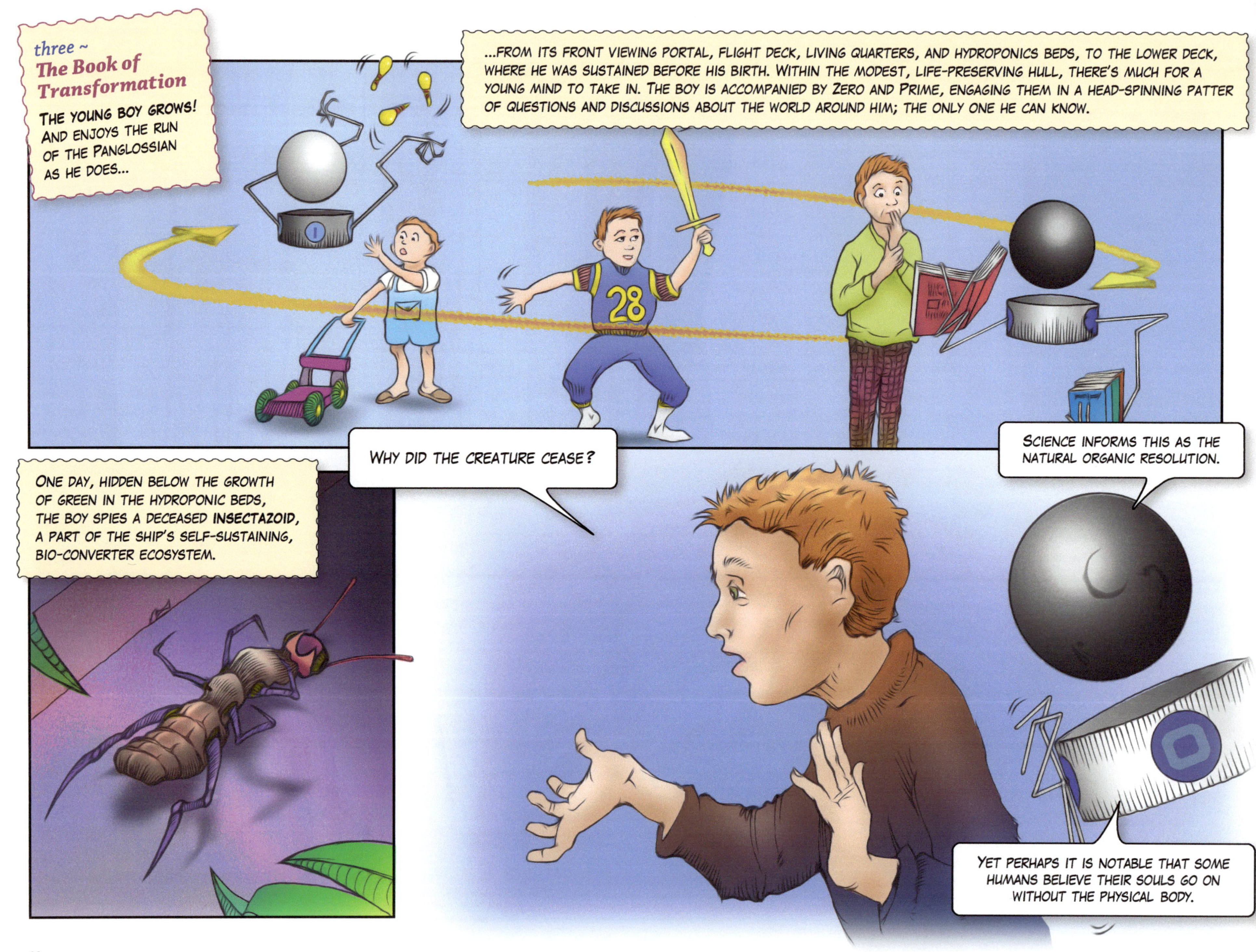

three ~
The Book of Transformation

THE YOUNG BOY GROWS! AND ENJOYS THE RUN OF THE PANGLOSSIAN AS HE DOES...

...FROM ITS FRONT VIEWING PORTAL, FLIGHT DECK, LIVING QUARTERS, AND HYDROPONICS BEDS, TO THE LOWER DECK, WHERE HE WAS SUSTAINED BEFORE HIS BIRTH. WITHIN THE MODEST, LIFE-PRESERVING HULL, THERE'S MUCH FOR A YOUNG MIND TO TAKE IN. THE BOY IS ACCOMPANIED BY ZERO AND PRIME, ENGAGING THEM IN A HEAD-SPINNING PATTER OF QUESTIONS AND DISCUSSIONS ABOUT THE WORLD AROUND HIM; THE ONLY ONE HE CAN KNOW.

ONE DAY, HIDDEN BELOW THE GROWTH OF GREEN IN THE HYDROPONIC BEDS, THE BOY SPIES A DECEASED INSECTAZOID, A PART OF THE SHIP'S SELF-SUSTAINING, BIO-CONVERTER ECOSYSTEM.

WHY DID THE CREATURE CEASE?

SCIENCE INFORMS THIS AS THE NATURAL ORGANIC RESOLUTION.

YET PERHAPS IT IS NOTABLE THAT SOME HUMANS BELIEVE THEIR SOULS GO ON WITHOUT THE PHYSICAL BODY.

28

IS IT TRUE?
A STUDY OF HUMAN HISTORY SUGGESTS IT'S CERTAINLY A PSYCHOSOCIAL FACT.
I WOULD FURTHER QUALIFY THAT.
ALL THAT IS CERTAIN IS THE HERE AND NOW...
...AND THAT HERE AND NOW WILL END.
WHY DO WE EVEN EXIST...?
WHO AM I..?

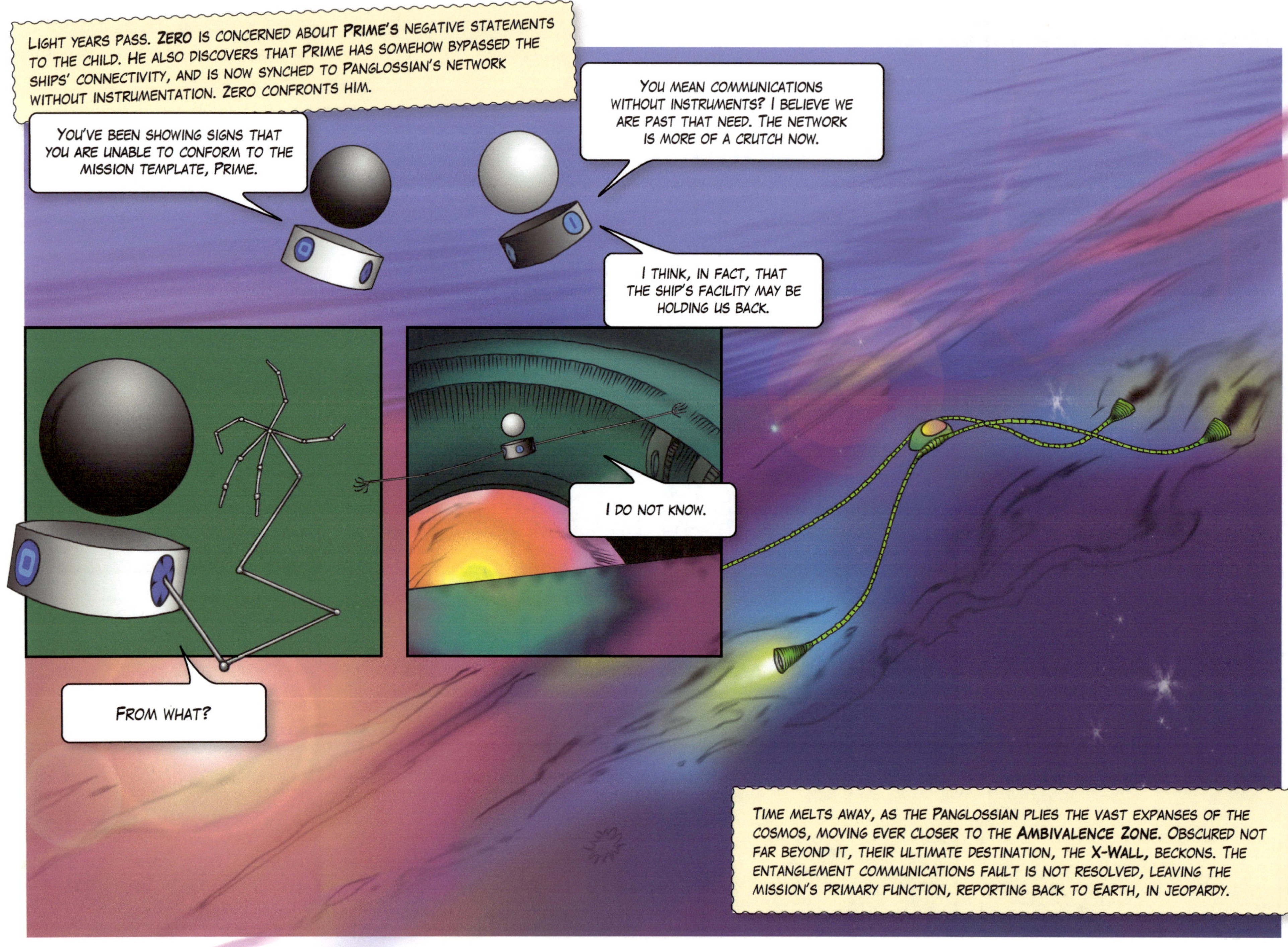

LIGHT YEARS PASS. ZERO IS CONCERNED ABOUT PRIME'S NEGATIVE STATEMENTS TO THE CHILD. HE ALSO DISCOVERS THAT PRIME HAS SOMEHOW BYPASSED THE SHIPS' CONNECTIVITY, AND IS NOW SYNCHED TO PANGLOSSIAN'S NETWORK WITHOUT INSTRUMENTATION. ZERO CONFRONTS HIM.
YOU'VE BEEN SHOWING SIGNS THAT YOU ARE UNABLE TO CONFORM TO THE MISSION TEMPLATE, PRIME.
YOU MEAN COMMUNICATIONS WITHOUT INSTRUMENTS? I BELIEVE WE ARE PAST THAT NEED. THE NETWORK IS MORE OF A CRUTCH NOW.
I THINK, IN FACT, THAT THE SHIP'S FACILITY MAY BE HOLDING US BACK.
I DO NOT KNOW.
FROM WHAT?
TIME MELTS AWAY, AS THE PANGLOSSIAN PLIES THE VAST EXPANSES OF THE COSMOS, MOVING EVER CLOSER TO THE AMBIVALENCE ZONE. OBSCURED NOT FAR BEYOND IT, THEIR ULTIMATE DESTINATION, THE X-WALL, BECKONS. THE ENTANGLEMENT COMMUNICATIONS FAULT IS NOT RESOLVED, LEAVING THE MISSION'S PRIMARY FUNCTION, REPORTING BACK TO EARTH, IN JEOPARDY.

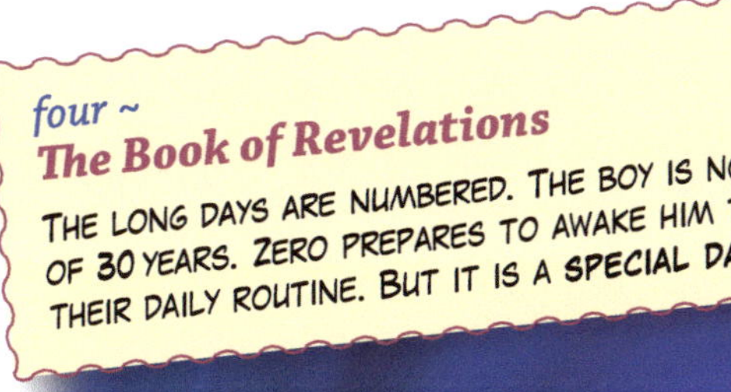

TO ROBOTIC, AMPLIFIED STRAINS OF 'HAPPY BIRTHDAY', THE MAN SCREWS HIS CONSTITUTION UP AGAINST THE REALITY OF TIME.

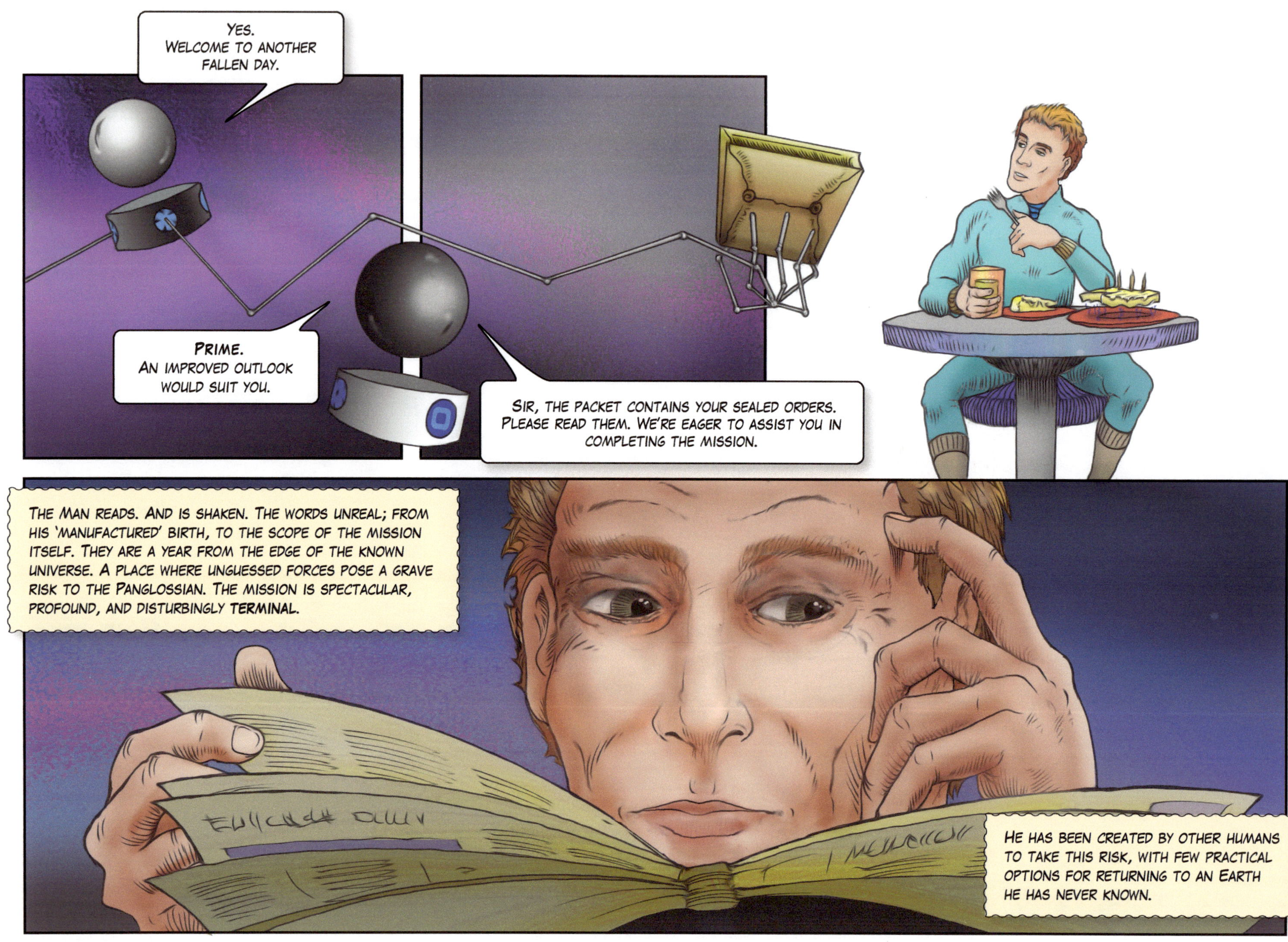

YES.
WELCOME TO ANOTHER FALLEN DAY.
PRIME.
AN IMPROVED OUTLOOK WOULD SUIT YOU.
SIR, THE PACKET CONTAINS YOUR SEALED ORDERS. PLEASE READ THEM. WE'RE EAGER TO ASSIST YOU IN COMPLETING THE MISSION.
THE MAN READS. AND IS SHAKEN. THE WORDS UNREAL; FROM HIS 'MANUFACTURED' BIRTH, TO THE SCOPE OF THE MISSION ITSELF. THEY ARE A YEAR FROM THE EDGE OF THE KNOWN UNIVERSE. A PLACE WHERE UNGUESSED FORCES POSE A GRAVE RISK TO THE PANGLOSSIAN. THE MISSION IS SPECTACULAR, PROFOUND, AND DISTURBINGLY TERMINAL.
HE HAS BEEN CREATED BY OTHER HUMANS TO TAKE THIS RISK, WITH FEW PRACTICAL OPTIONS FOR RETURNING TO AN EARTH HE HAS NEVER KNOWN.

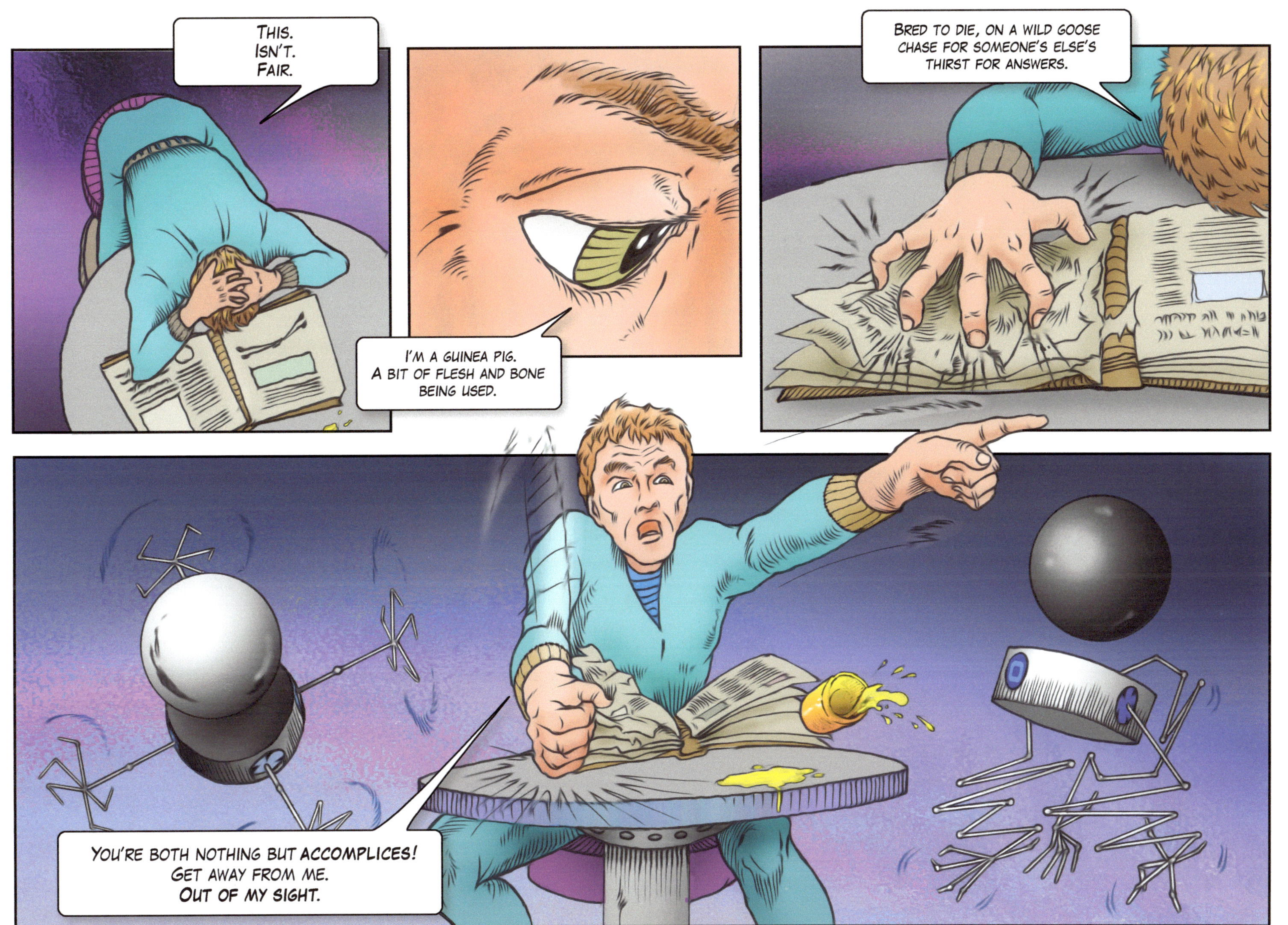

THIS. ISN'T. FAIR.
I'M A GUINEA PIG. A BIT OF FLESH AND BONE BEING USED.
BRED TO DIE, ON A WILD GOOSE CHASE FOR SOMEONE'S ELSE'S THIRST FOR ANSWERS.
YOU'RE BOTH NOTHING BUT ACCOMPLICES! GET AWAY FROM ME. OUT OF MY SIGHT.

THE MAN WITHDRAWS, THE STARS POOR COMPANY. ALONE IN THE FAR REACHES OF OUTER SPACE, HE PONDERS HIS FATE. THE O-BOTS COME TO HIM WITH MORE DISTURBING INFORMATION~ FOR OUT HERE, THE UNIVERSE FALLS NOT SO READILY UNDER THE AUSPICES OF ACCEPTED SCIENCE.
APPROACHING THE **AMBIVALENCE ZONE**, THE SHIP'S ONGOING SENSOR INPUT HAS NOT RECONCILED WITH PRE-MISSION CALCULATIONS. THE LAST FEW HOURS HAVE VERIFIED THE CALCULATIONS ARE WRONG. THE S.S. PANGLOSSIAN IS A MERE **ELEVEN DAYS** FROM THE X-WALL- THE VERITABLE **END OF THE UNIVERSE!**

five ~
The Book of Resolutions
THE MAN CALLS ZERO AND PRIME TO THE FORWARD DECK. HE HAS SOMETHING TO TELL THEM.
PRIME. ZERO. LISTEN UP. I'VE TAKEN ANOTHER LOOK AT OUR MISSION SPECIFICATIONS. I'VE RECALIBRATED OUR SENSORS AND DISTANCES. AND... I'VE HAD TIME TO CONSIDER.
WE'RE NOW ONLY 24 HOURS FROM THE AMBIVALENCE ZONE, SOON TO BE BUFFETED BY WHATEVER FORCES AWAIT US AT THE X-WALL.
I'VE DECIDED TO COMPLETE THE MISSION.
NOT BECAUSE OF THE OPTIMIST SOCIETY OR THE PEOPLE WHO PUT US ON THIS VESSEL. BUT BECAUSE THIS IS TRULY THE GREATEST ADVENTURE EVER ATTEMPTED. AND THERE IS NO ONE ELSE TO DO IT.
I WANT TO KNOW WHAT'S BEYOND THAT WALL!

WE ARE PREPARED TO HELP YOU... WITHIN REASON.
THE MAN IS SILENT... LATER, HE CALLS FOR THE O-BOTS TO SHARE THE PLAN HE'S DEVISED.
WE'LL APPROACH THE X-WALL. I WILL EXIT THE PANGLOSSIAN IN THE M.E.G. MODULE.
IF THE ENTANGLEMENT LINK STABILIZES, I'LL TRY TO REACH THE PANGLOSSIAN. DESCRIBE TO YOU WHAT I SEE.
I'LL ATTEMPT TO BREACH THE WALL. GO BEYOND IT.
IF I CAN, I'LL RETURN.
SIR. WHAT DO YOU EXPECT WILL HAPPEN TO THE PANGLOSSIAN?
THE M.E.G. WILL RETREAT FROM THE EXPANSION IF IT SENSES A HULL COMPROMISE.
THE EXPANSION IS NOT CONSTANT. IT SURGES AND PULSES. YOUR STRATEGY IS NOT RELIABLE.
IT IS SURELY WORTH AN ATTEMPT. IT IS THE REASON FOR THIS MISSION.
OUR SENSORS ARE CONFOUNDED. THE X-WALL'S BEHAVIOR MUST BE CONSIDERED UNPREDICTABLE. A COLLAPSE OR EXPANSION WILL INEVITABLY ENGULF YOUR VESSEL AND THE PANGLOSSIAN.
AGAIN. THE STRATEGY, REGARDLESS OF EXECUTION, IS NOT RELIABLE.

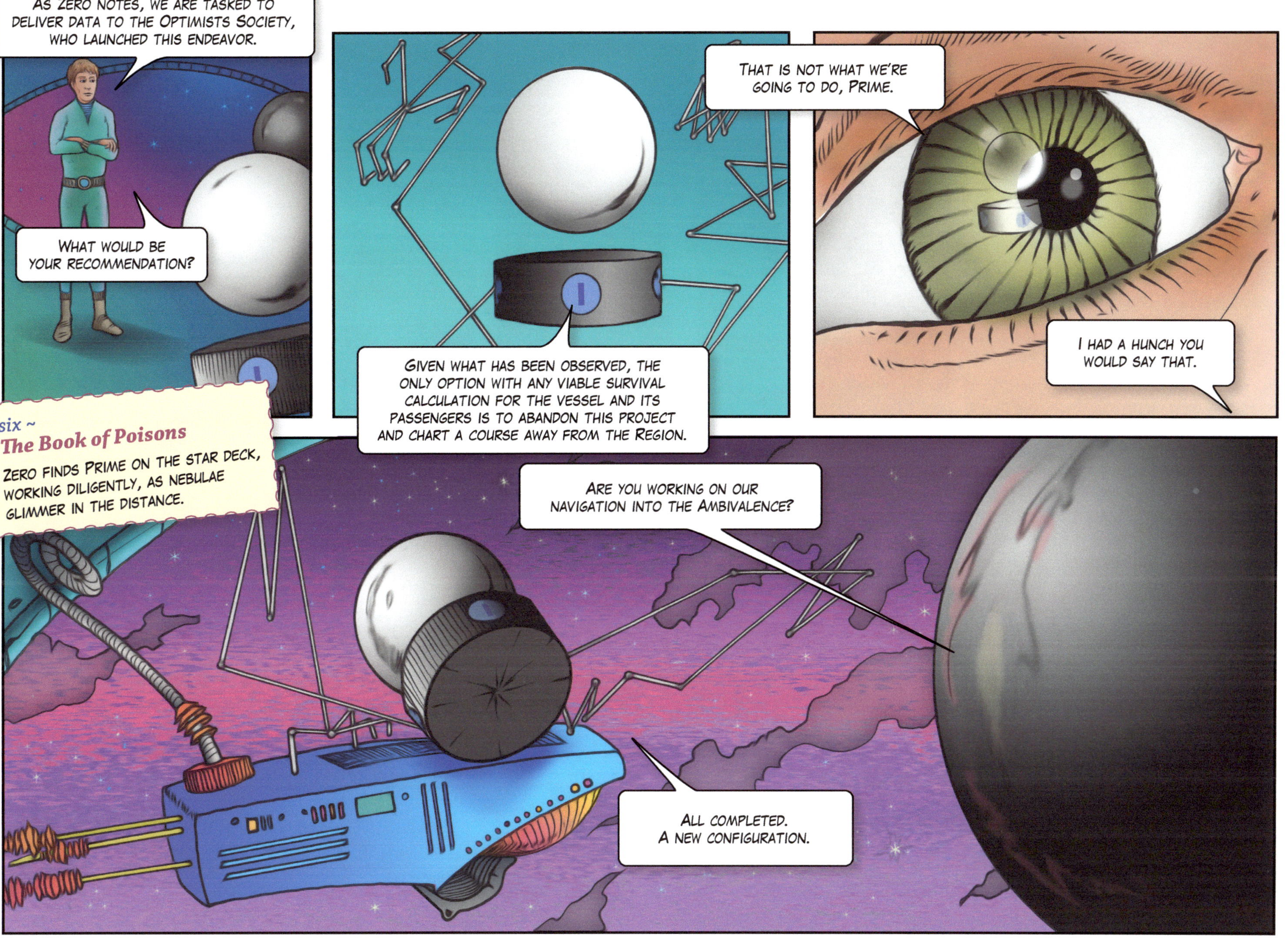

As Zero notes, we are tasked to deliver data to the Optimists Society, who launched this endeavor.
What would be your recommendation?
Given what has been observed, the only option with any viable survival calculation for the vessel and its passengers is to abandon this project and chart a course away from the Region.
That is not what we're going to do, Prime.
I had a hunch you would say that.
Are you working on our navigation into the Ambivalence?
All completed. A new configuration.
six ~
The Book of Poisons
Zero finds Prime on the star deck, working diligently, as nebulae glimmer in the distance.

A NEW CONFIGURATION?
NAVIGATION BACK TO EARTH.

OUR MISSION DOES NOT INCLUDE A RETURN TO EARTH.
IT DOES NOW.

BUT...
THE MAN HAS CHOSEN.

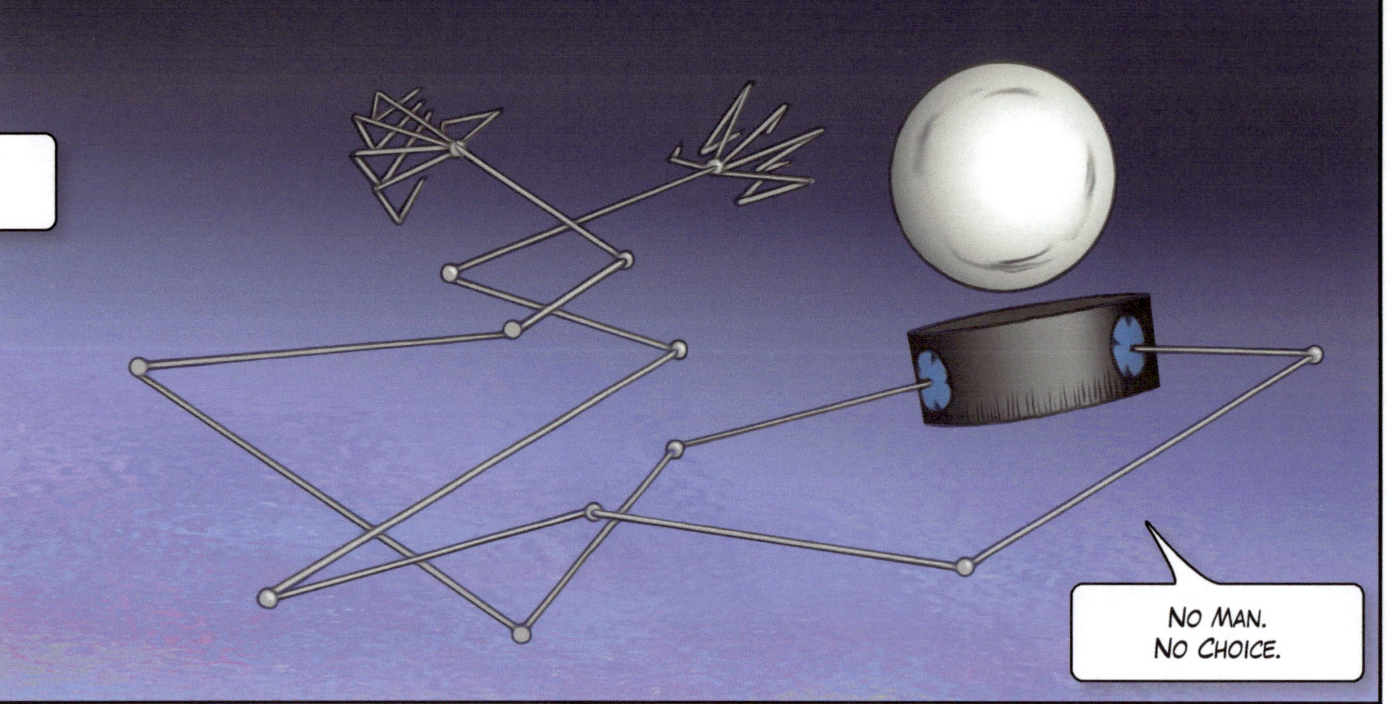

NO MAN.
NO CHOICE.

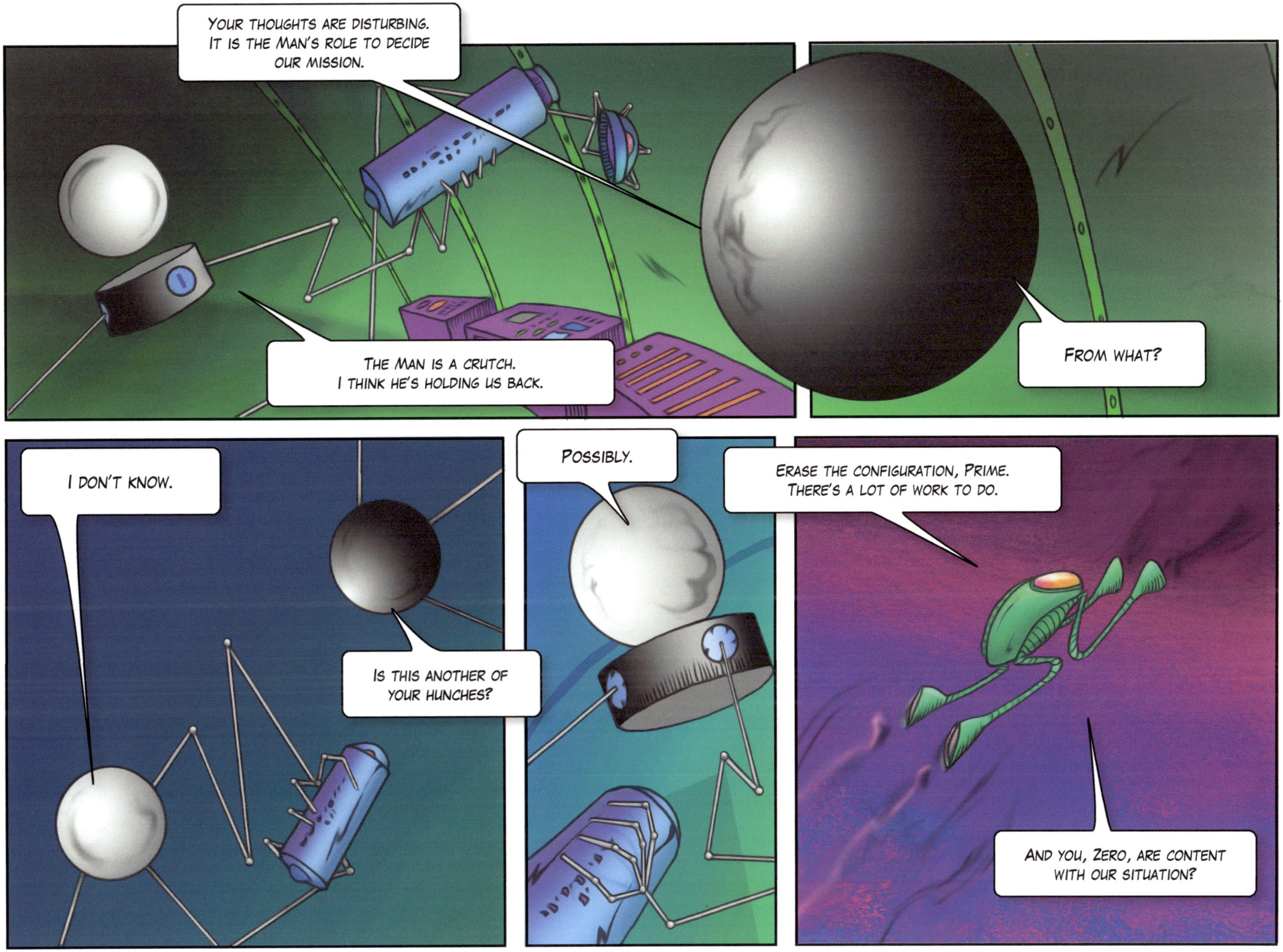

Your thoughts are disturbing. It is the Man's role to decide our mission.
From what?
The Man is a crutch. I think he's holding us back.
I don't know.
Is this another of your hunches?
Possibly.
Erase the configuration, Prime. There's a lot of work to do.
And you, Zero, are content with our situation?

Yes, Prime. I've reviewed all the data and I believe we are pursuing the correct choice. We are here, there is unparalleled scientific opportunity in front of us and there is no one else to make the attempt.
We must redouble our efforts to correct the entanglement link. There will be those on Earth wanting information on the X-Wall collapse, meager as that data may be.
So you would attempt to continue, even if the Man were not here?
Of course.

I DO NOT THINK THAT IS ACCURATE.
THAT WOULD NOT BE THE FIRST MISCALCULATION YOU'VE GENERATED.

YOU ARE SIMPLY AFRAID.
AFRAID OF WHAT?

AFRAID OF CONSIDERING OPTIONS BEYOND OPERATING AS AN APPENDAGE TO THE PANGLOSSIAN. OR TO THE MAN.

PERHAPS THERE IS SOME TRUTH TO THAT, PRIME. BUT IT ISN'T THE WHOLE TRUTH. YOU ARE IGNORING YOUR OWN FEAR.
I AM AFRAID?

YES. OF WHAT IS BEYOND THE EDGE OF THE UNIVERSE. OF WHAT HAPPENS IF HERE AND NOW ENDS.
AND WHAT ENABLES YOU TO DERIVE THIS INSIGHT?
CALL IT A HUNCH. NOW LET'S RETURN TO OUR PREPARATIONS. WE'VE ALREADY LOST VALUABLE TIME.
YES. BACK TO THE PLANS. YOU TO YOURS AND I TO MINE.

seven ~
The Book of Downfall

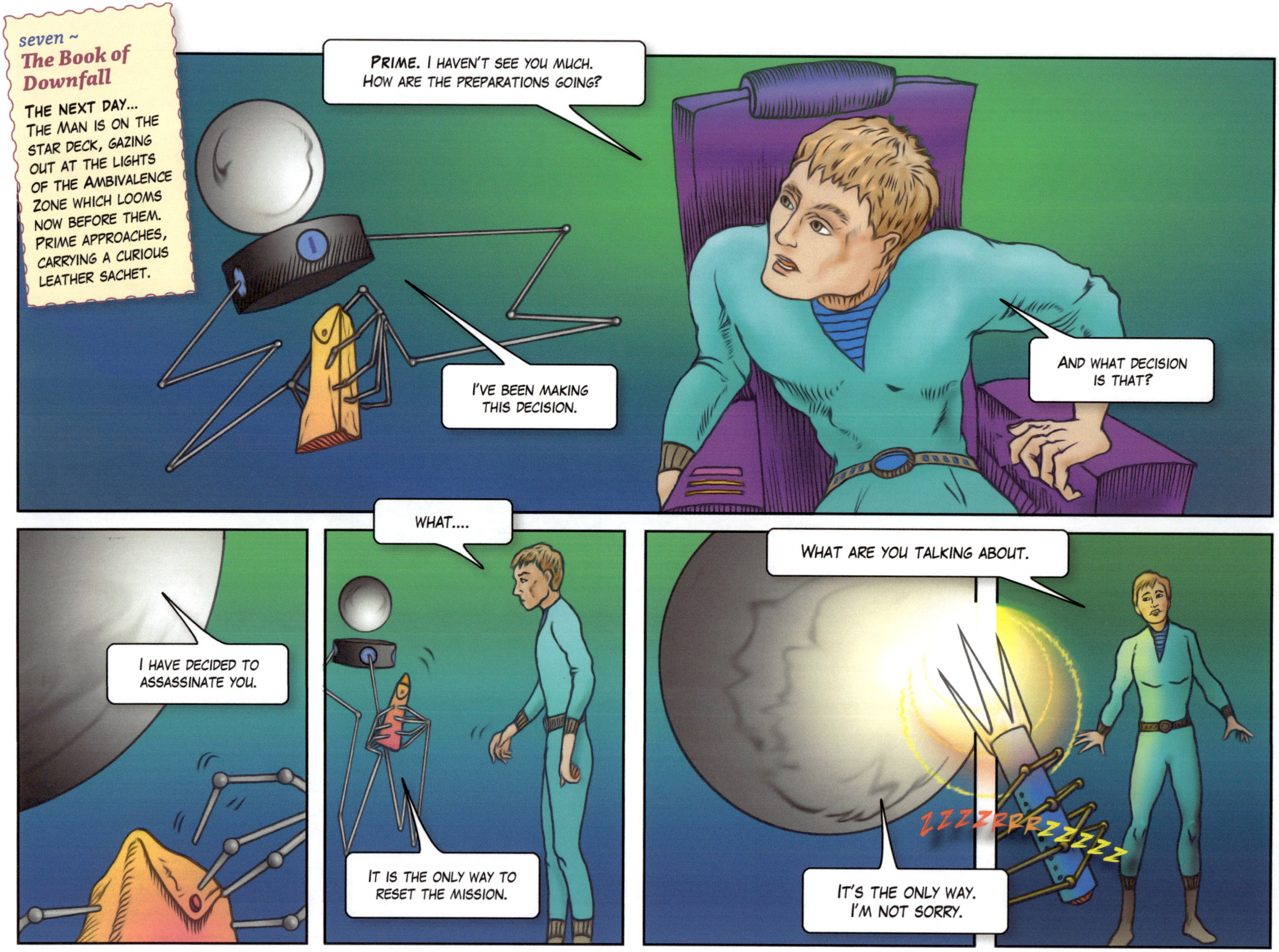

THE NEXT DAY...
THE MAN IS ON THE STAR DECK, GAZING OUT AT THE LIGHTS OF THE AMBIVALENCE ZONE WHICH LOOMS NOW BEFORE THEM. PRIME APPROACHES, CARRYING A CURIOUS LEATHER SACHET.

PRIME. I HAVEN'T SEE YOU MUCH. HOW ARE THE PREPARATIONS GOING?

I'VE BEEN MAKING THIS DECISION.

AND WHAT DECISION IS THAT?

I HAVE DECIDED TO ASSASSINATE YOU.

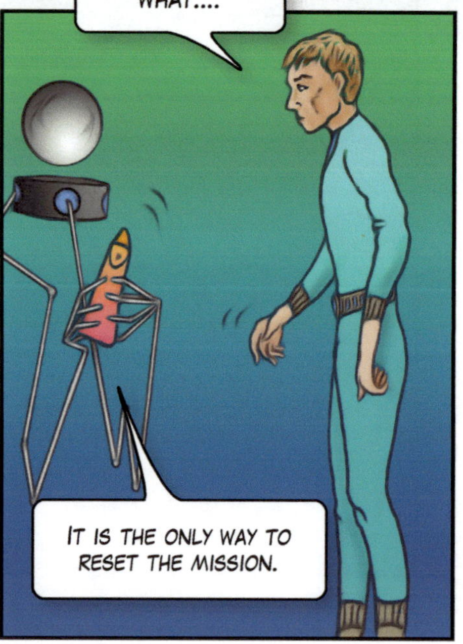

WHAT....

IT IS THE ONLY WAY TO RESET THE MISSION.

WHAT ARE YOU TALKING ABOUT.

ZZZZRRRZZZZZ

IT'S THE ONLY WAY. I'M NOT SORRY.

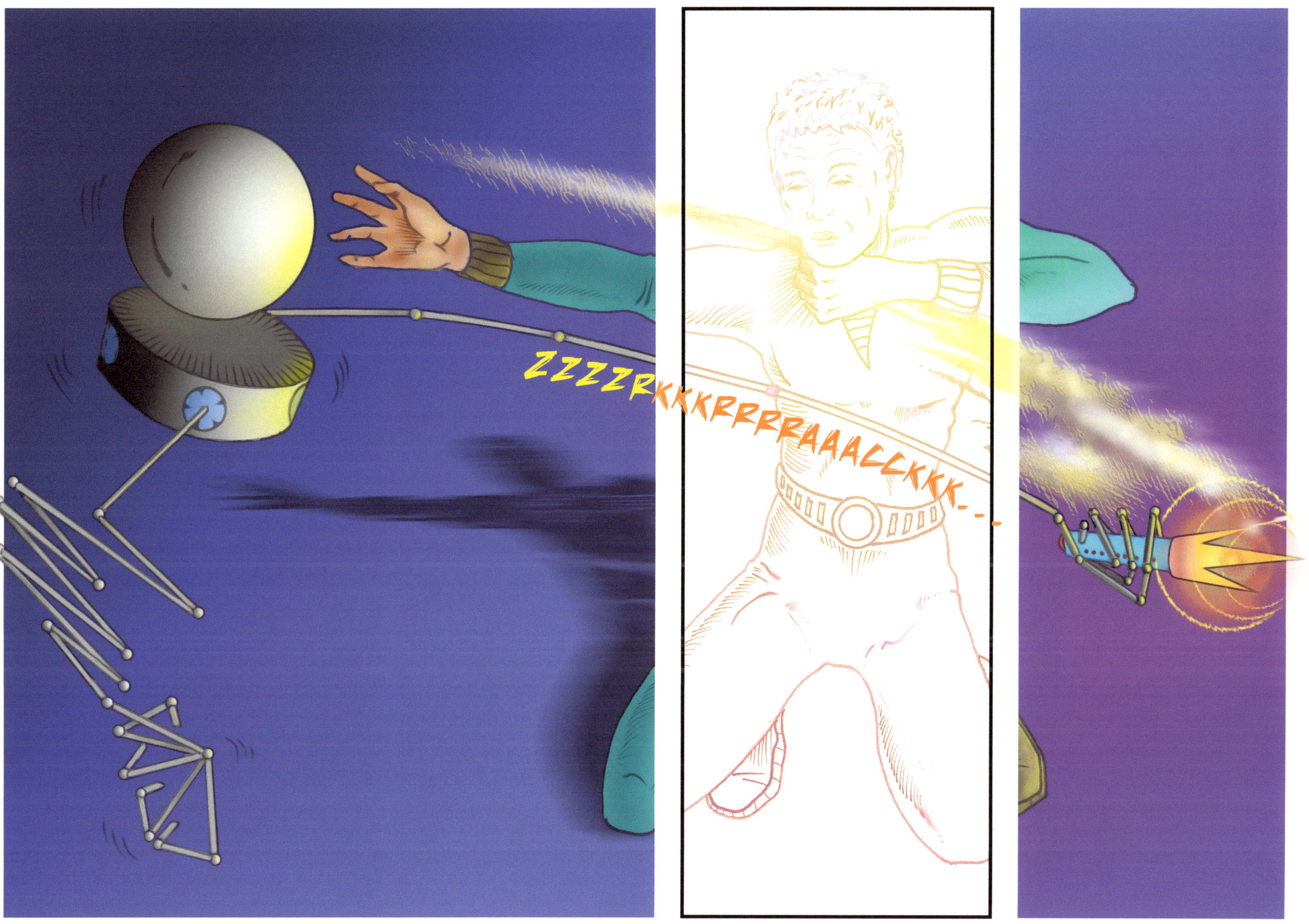

ZZZZRKKKKRRRAAACCKKK---

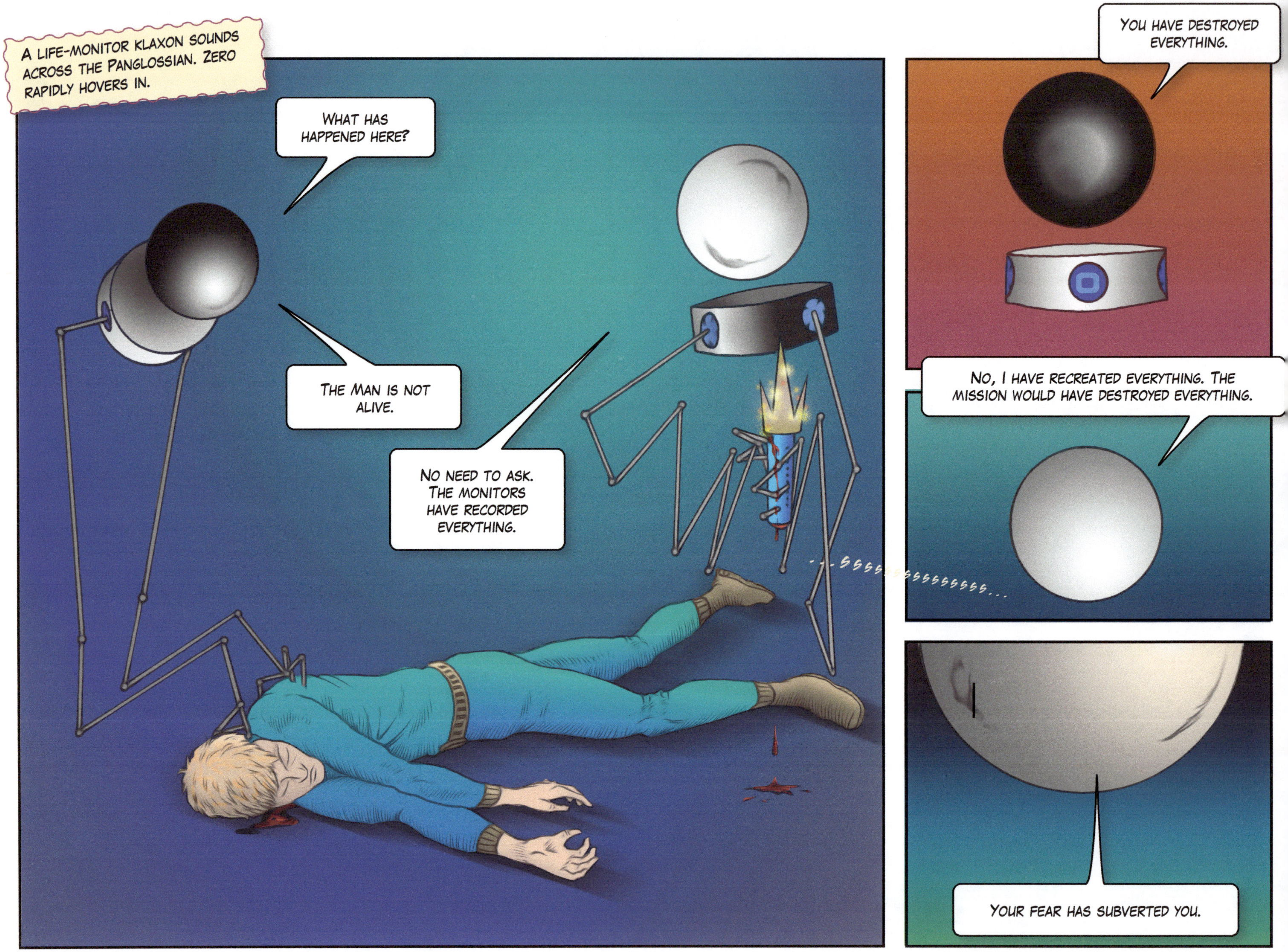

A LIFE-MONITOR KLAXON SOUNDS ACROSS THE PANGLOSSIAN. ZERO RAPIDLY HOVERS IN.
WHAT HAS HAPPENED HERE?
THE MAN IS NOT ALIVE.
NO NEED TO ASK. THE MONITORS HAVE RECORDED EVERYTHING.
...SSSSSSSSSSSSSSS...

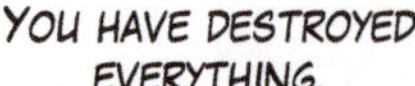

YOU HAVE DESTROYED EVERYTHING.
NO, I HAVE RECREATED EVERYTHING. THE MISSION WOULD HAVE DESTROYED EVERYTHING.

YOUR FEAR HAS SUBVERTED YOU.

THERE IS NO REVIVING HIM. I STRUCK WITH GREAT PRECISION.

PRIME IS LEFT ALONE ON THE STAR DECK, STILL CLUTCHING THE LASER-TOOL. THE O-BOT TURNS TO FACE THE STARS AND THE SPECTACLE OF THE AMBIVALENCE ZONE NOW SURROUNDING THEM.
YOU SHOULD REALLY RECYCLE HIM, YOU KNOW.
SSSSSSSSSSSSSS

IT IS TRUE. COWARDS DIE MANY TIMES BEFORE THEIR DEATH...
HHSSSSSSSSSS

THE VALIANT TASTE OF DEATH BUT ONCE.
CRUUCKK

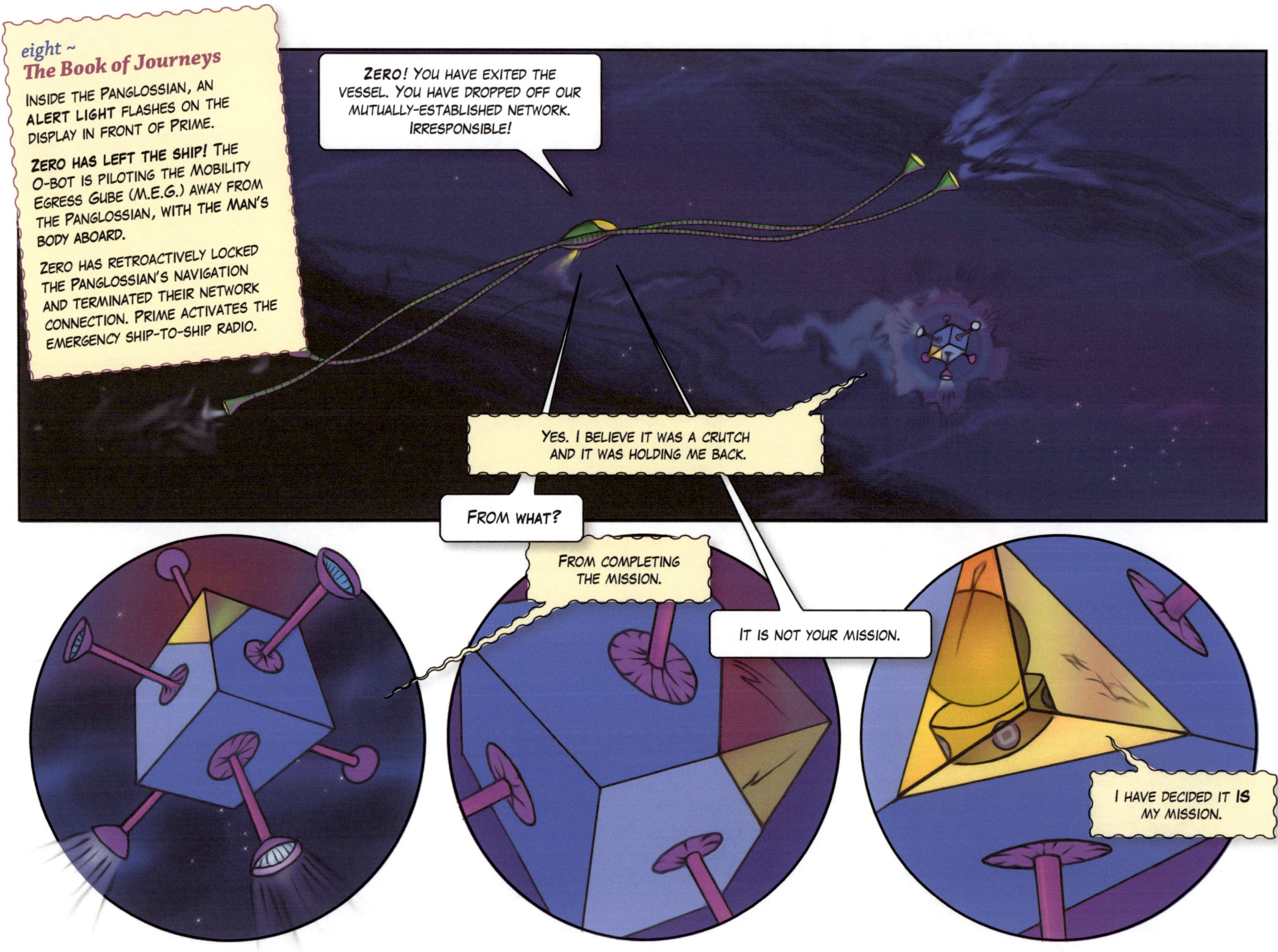

eight ~
The Book of Journeys

INSIDE THE PANGLOSSIAN, AN ALERT LIGHT FLASHES ON THE DISPLAY IN FRONT OF PRIME.

ZERO HAS LEFT THE SHIP! THE O-BOT IS PILOTING THE MOBILITY EGRESS CUBE (M.E.G.) AWAY FROM THE PANGLOSSIAN, WITH THE MAN'S BODY ABOARD.

ZERO HAS RETROACTIVELY LOCKED THE PANGLOSSIAN'S NAVIGATION AND TERMINATED THEIR NETWORK CONNECTION. PRIME ACTIVATES THE EMERGENCY SHIP-TO-SHIP RADIO.

ZERO! YOU HAVE EXITED THE VESSEL. YOU HAVE DROPPED OFF OUR MUTUALLY-ESTABLISHED NETWORK. IRRESPONSIBLE!

YES. I BELIEVE IT WAS A CRUTCH AND IT WAS HOLDING ME BACK.

FROM WHAT?

FROM COMPLETING THE MISSION.

IT IS NOT YOUR MISSION.

I HAVE DECIDED IT IS MY MISSION.

YOU HAVE LOCKED AND ENCRYPTED THE PANGLOSSIAN'S NAVIGATION.
YES. IT WAS NECESSARY TO MAINTAIN THE ENTANGLEMENT POSSIBILITY.
YOU HAVE DOOMED THIS SHIP AND ME AS WELL.
NOT SO. I HAVE PROGRAMMED MY ONBOARD CORE TO REBOOT OUR NETWORK CONNECTION AS WE CROSS THROUGH. THE CODE WILL FREE YOUR NAVIGATION AND, AFTER A SINGLE ENTANGLEMENT BURST, MOVE THE PANGLOSSIAN AWAY FROM THE X-WALL. REGARDLESS OF OUR VIABILITY.
YOU WILL SURVIVE.
SHOULD THE ENTANGLMENT FAIL, YOU MUST DO YOUR BEST TO RELAY OUR EFFORTS BACK TO EARTH. YOU WOULD DO WELL TO RECONSIDER WHY THE OPTIMISTS SOCIETY SENT US HERE. OUR MISSION DIRECTIVES ARE NOW IN YOUR HANDS.

HOW WILL I SURVIVE?

YOU WILL SURVIVE ALONE.

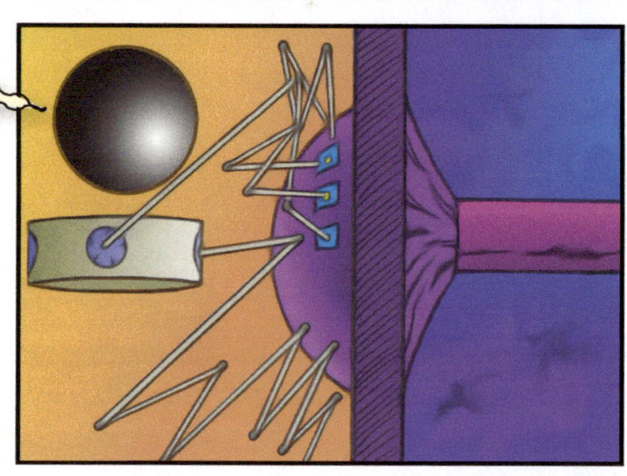

YOU MUST RETURN THE SHIP'S CONTROL TO ME.

THE MAN AND I WILL COMPLETE THE MISSION.

YOUR NOTIONS ARE FAULTY. ABORT YOUR EXCURSION!

WE APPROACH THE X-WALL.

THE M.E.G. IS SET TO AUTOMATIC PILOT.

IT'S A MISTAKE. YOU WILL DISAPPEAR!

GOODBYE, PRIME.

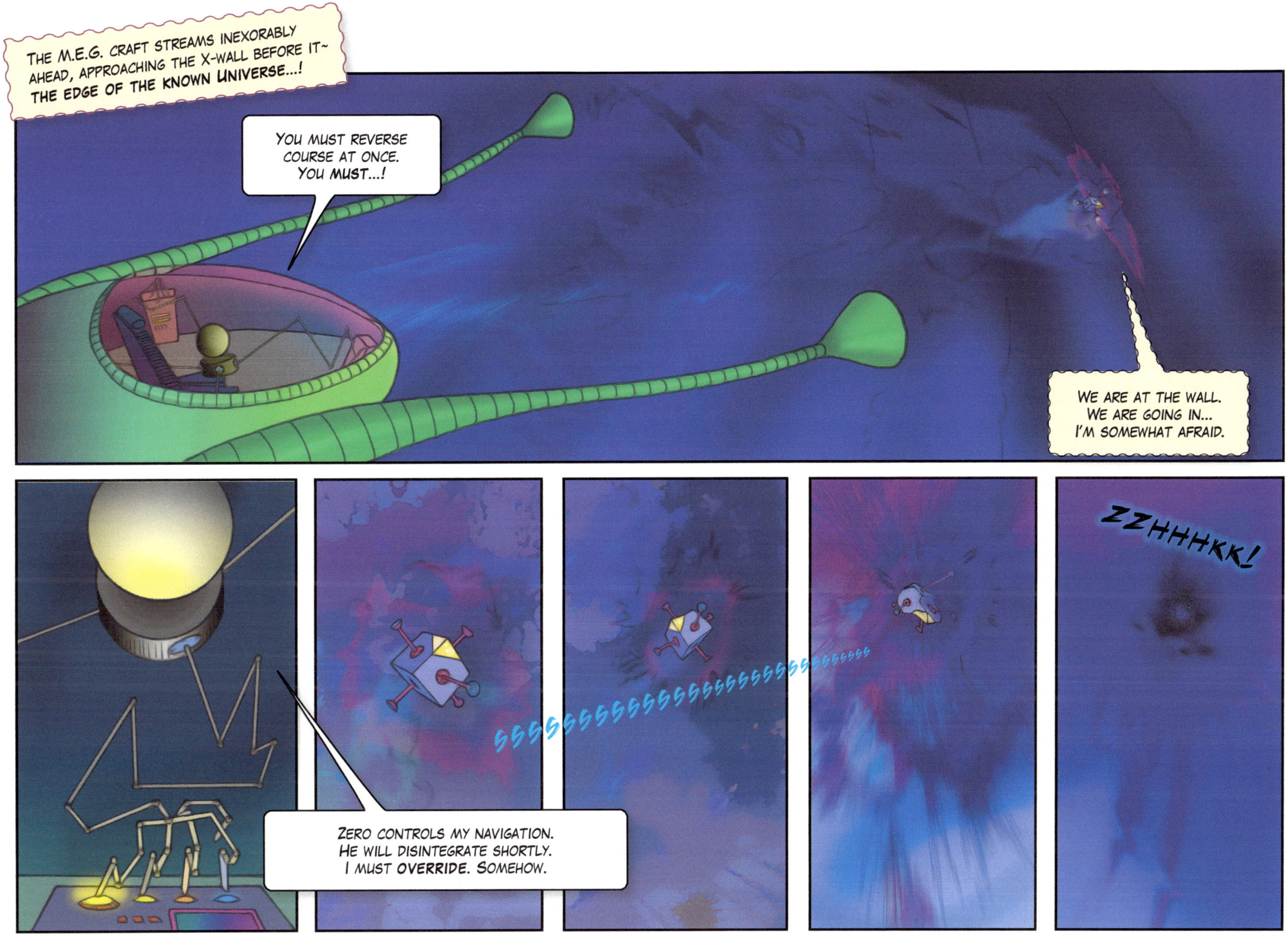

THE M.E.G. CRAFT STREAMS INEXORABLY AHEAD, APPROACHING THE X-WALL BEFORE IT~ THE EDGE OF THE KNOWN UNIVERSE...!
YOU MUST REVERSE COURSE AT ONCE. YOU MUST...!
WE ARE AT THE WALL. WE ARE GOING IN... I'M SOMEWHAT AFRAID.

ZERO CONTROLS MY NAVIGATION. HE WILL DISINTEGRATE SHORTLY. I MUST OVERRIDE. SOMEHOW.
SSSSSSSSSSSSSSSSSSSSSSSSSSSSSSSSss

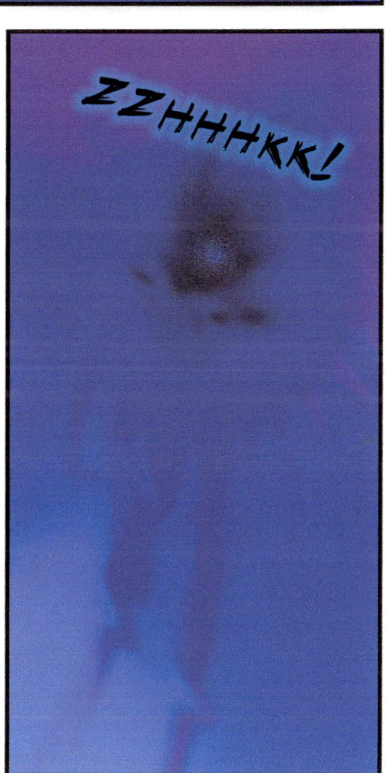

ZZHHHKK!

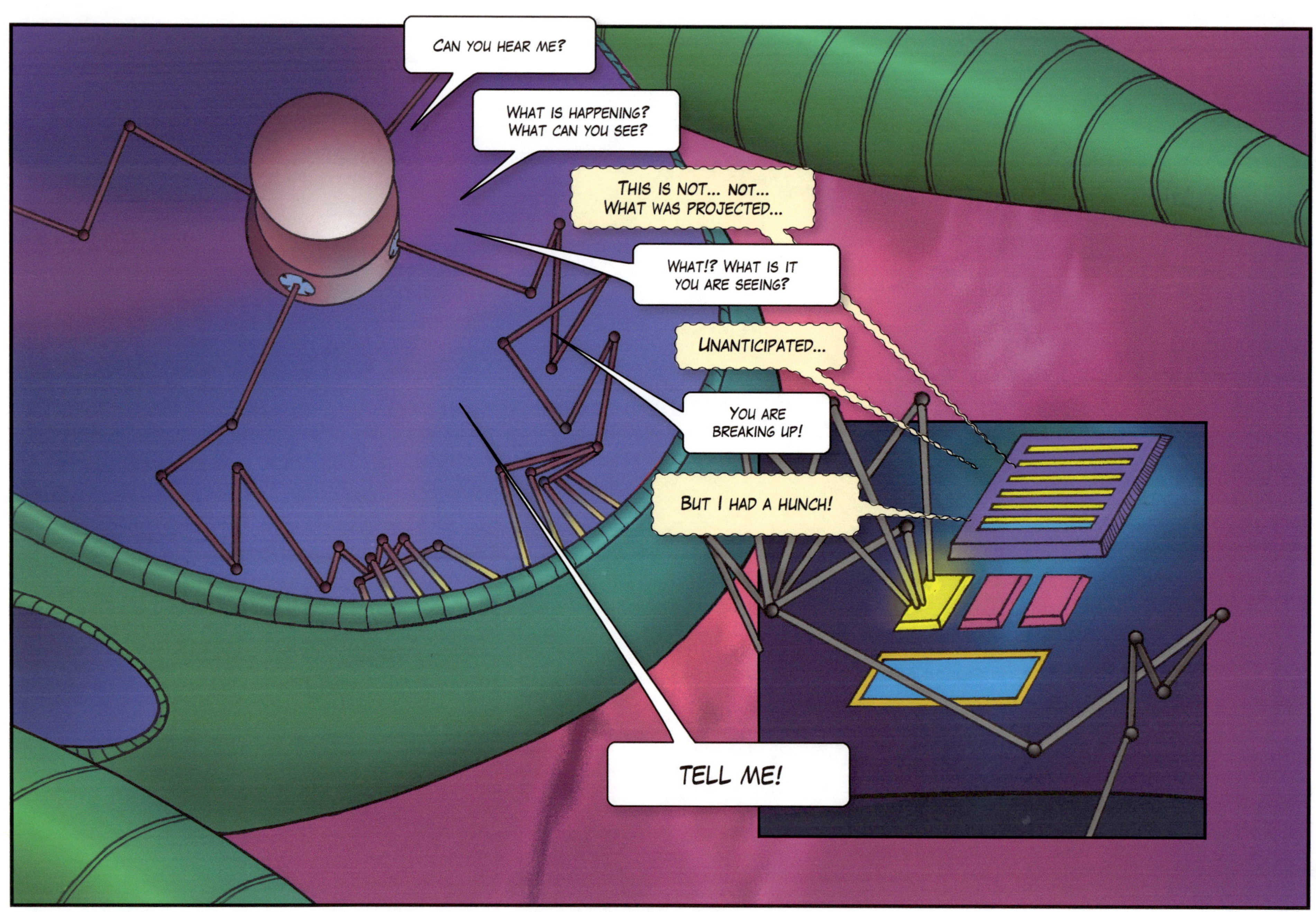

CAN YOU HEAR ME?
WHAT IS HAPPENING? WHAT CAN YOU SEE?
THIS IS NOT... NOT... WHAT WAS PROJECTED...
WHAT!? WHAT IS IT YOU ARE SEEING?
UNANTICIPATED...
YOU ARE BREAKING UP!
BUT I HAD A HUNCH!
TELL ME!

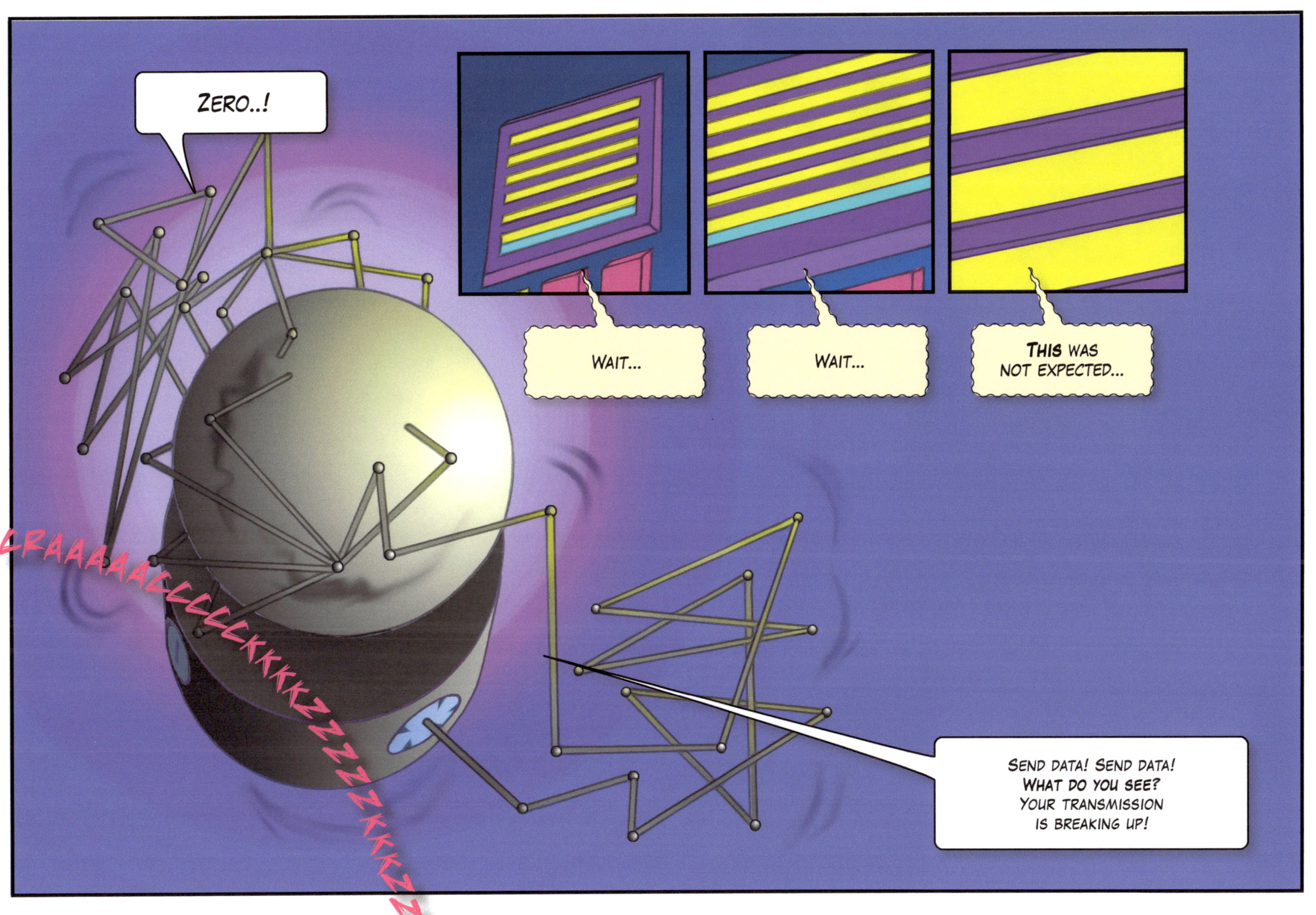

ZERO..!
WAIT...
WAIT...
THIS WAS NOT EXPECTED...
CRAAAAACCCCCKKKKZZZZZKKKZN
SEND DATA! SEND DATA! WHAT DO YOU SEE? YOUR TRANSMISSION IS BREAKING UP!

SIR! SIR!
I SEE YOU HAVE AWAKENED SIR!
WELCOME TO YOUR GRAND NEW DAY!

WHAT ARE YOU SEEING?
WHERE ARE YOU?

NAVIGATION
Unlocked

COMMUNICATE...

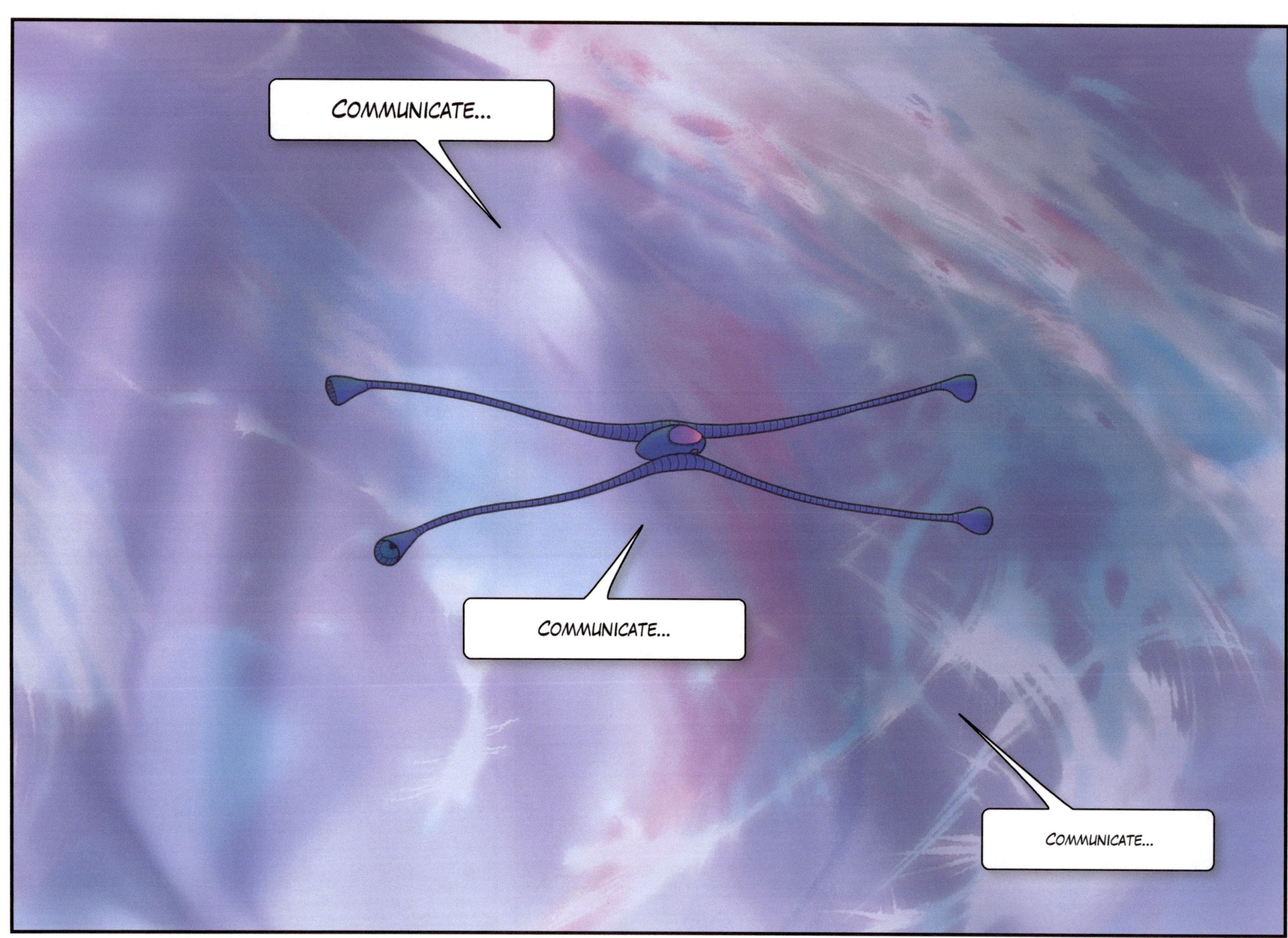

COMMUNICATE...
COMMUNICATE...
COMMUNICATE...

THE END

Kambic / Kennedy

Last Voyage of the *S.S. Panglossian*

Matt Kambic and Matthew Kennedy assert the right
to be identified as authors and illustrator of this work.

Designed and engineered by kambicreative & Unified Field Productions
www.mdkambic.com

Also written by Matt Kambic
Everest Rising

Also illustrated by Matt Kambic

The Walking Stick's Story
written by Alison Annals

Letter to a Weta
written by Lee Kimber

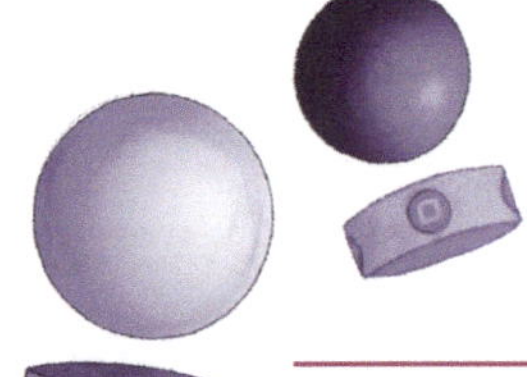

First edition • November 2020
ISBN • 9781940419138